I dedicate these books to my three AWESOME children:
Chloe, Tyler, and Jake!

I also dedicate these books to anyone and everyone seeking
something bigger and better!
Watch it happen!

This is Level 2 for *FIND SOMETHING AWESOME!* The idea was to create a needed modern *Aesop's Fables* as bedtime stories from parent to child.

The "fables" are stories to introduce and develop the listener's own capabilities: imagination, self-confidence, positivity, and ultimate success and happiness. I have more levels that follow to introduce a child to how his/her brain works in this world.

To my knowledge, there are no such manuals in this capacity, for young children. I've discovered things our brains are capable of in this world, good and bad. With three children of my own, I don't want them to have to re-invent the wheel.

In my experience with teaching these messages/capabilities to my kids and their friends, I have found they are capable of understanding, asking great questions, and most importantly, using them in daily life/challenges and are eager to learn more! It's been amazing!

Each story will be followed by some relevant questions and of course, by each capability and step.

Each time I read these, the kids always ask, "What is our capability?" and, "What is our step?" It's their favorite part. And then questions and discussions always ensue. It makes for great parent/child communication.

I hope you discover the "miracle" we live in...

www.mascotbooks.com

Have You Ever Thanked a Rainbow?

©2016 Matt Scott. All Rights Reserved. No part of this publication may be reproduced, stored in a retrieval system or transmitted in any form by any means electronic, mechanical, or photocopying, recording or otherwise without the permission of the author.

For more information, please contact:
Mascot Books
560 Herndon Parkway #120
Herndon, VA 20170
info@mascotbooks.com

Library of Congress Control Number: 2016905696

CPSIA Code: PRT0516A
ISBN: 978-1-63177-486-7

Printed in the United States

Have You Ever Thanked a Rainbow?

by **Matt Scott**
art by **Ana Sebastian**

Good morning! Good morning! Open your eyes!
Stretch out your arms up into the skies!

What are you going to DO today? What are you going to BE?
For everything is a miracle I'll show you, you'll see!

Your thoughts, they can go ANY which way!
And right here before you is a brand new WHOLE day!

Twenty-four hours, this day it will last.
So inflate your chest and let's get to the task!

'Cause your brain needs this air so thoughts can stay high!
And thoughts find your world from the earth to your eye!

So in this new day what SHOULD we DO?
What should we BE? Do YOU have a clue?

FIND AWESOME THINGS! That's what I say!
But that's just step one, to teach, if I may...

Look or listen as you breathe deep within.
Or touch with your hand something neat on your skin.

Find something awesome whichever which way.
Five senses to use to SEEK on this day!

Each second you live it's YOUR job to find
the thoughts in your head that come from your mind!

Find awesome! Find awesome! is what you should ask.
Set this thought in your mind to this realizing task.

Now be careful!

Some steps you take could lead to not getting.
Interference, this is, but no need to be fretting!

Just take a deep breath and stay focused on finding!
'Cause awesome just needs more time for unwinding!

While taking more steps repeat in your head,
"I can and it will," and **BELIEVE** in what's said!

Something awesome WILL come! If "find" is your "do".
A promise this is, I assure you, it's true!

So today, "finding awesome" we'll set out to DO,
but then how we'll BE comes next with step two!

Once awesome comes, then how will we **BE**?
There's only one answer to continue the see!

Be thankful, be thankful, and watch what it does!
You're happy! So happy, and not just because!

A thing that you thank gives back something too.
Our world's cool design, as Newton once knew.

These steps are for real, but take practice to master.
The more that you try your happy comes faster.

The easiest of tests, to prove, if you dare,
is after the rain, look up in the air!

With your mind seeking awesome I hope you do see,
a rainbow before you above a green tree!

Step one is accomplished as promised, too true!
But thanking you must as described in step two!

So thanking a rainbow is something to try.
Seek awesome! Be thankful! I hope you see why!

QUESTIONS

What are you going to DO right now?

What is a good thing for you to say to yourself if you haven't found anything awesome yet?

What are you going to BE when you find something awesome?

Why do you thank things?

Can you find something awesome?

CAPABILITIES

Keep your brain focused on positive things!

Find awesomeness!

Be thankful!

Be happy!

STEPS

Find awesome things, always!

Thank them, and be thankful!

Be sure to check out:
FIND SOMETHING AWESOME!
Level 3: Did You Laugh When You Stubbed Your Toe?

ABOUT THE AUTHOR

Matt grew up in Montana and moved to Southern California when he was twenty-four years old. Leaving his "newly discovered security blanket of friends and family behind," he recognized he needed to find and develop his own voice and confidence in this "new" and challenging world.

During this search he became an active believer and dedicated reader of success and self-help books, claiming, "Some were good, some were bad, but most had similar messages."

He proclaims to have become a successful and happy person, husband, father, businessman, and friend due to practicing the steps created from the information in these similar messages.

Matt knows these messages are things EVERYONE'S brains are capable of doing, and are, in fact, the "secrets" to success and happiness.

Now with three children of his own, he was shocked he could not find anything to communicate these "secrets" to his children, despite the thousands of options and variations for adults.

Matt was inspired to create *FIND SOMETHING AWESOME!* a book series to introduce and communicate these messages and capabilities in a fun and universal approach for this younger audience.

The stories provide an introduction to imagination, positivity, mind, ego, self-confidence, pitfalls, and more. With these introductions, the stories also ultimately provide steps for success and happiness.

In Matt's own words, it's already been a rewarding undertaking.

"In my experience with teaching these messages/capabilities to my kids and their friends, I have found they are capable of understanding, asking great questions, and most importantly, using them in daily life/challenges and are eager to learn more! It's been amazing!

"Each time I read these, at the end of each story the kids always ask, 'What is our capability?' and, 'What is our step?' It's their favorite part...and then questions and discussions always ensue. It makes for great parent/child communication.

"Each story will be followed by some relevant questions and of course, by each capability and step. I hope you all utilize this information and discover the 'miracle' we live in! Miracles are awesome!"

- Matt Scott